This book belongs to:

....

....

Written by Kath Smith
Illustrated by Caroline Jayne Church
Language consultant: Betty Root

This is a Parragon Publishing book
This edition published in 2005

Parragon Publishing
Queen Street House
4 Queen Street
Bath BA1 1HE, UK

ISBN 1-40544-786-9

The Little Friends

Princesses are Pretty

p

Snoozy Princess Susie

Princess Susie was quite perfect
In almost every way.
She always fed her dragon, Spark,
And put her clothes away.

She never ever said bad words,
Or disobeyed the queen.
Her bedroom was the tidiest
That you have ever seen!

But Susie did do something
That made her mother weep.
No matter what the time of day,
Poor Susie fell asleep!

She fell asleep at breakfast time,
And snored in the banquet hall.
She often dozed upon the stairs,
All curled up in a ball.

Z-Z-Z-Z-Z

The queen was just beside herself.
"The answer's plain," she said.
"If Susie cannot stay awake,
She must go straight to bed!"

But though she went to bed at six,
And didn't rise till nine,
Susie yawned and snored all day,
No matter what the time.

No one knew just what to do,
To put the matter right,
Till clever Fairy Heather saw
Something strange one night.

As she flew home in the dark
She heard a gentle sigh.
There was Susie, wide awake,
Gazing at the sky!

"I love to watch the stars," she said,
"And see the shining moon!
I'd rather be here, counting stars,
Than sleeping in *my* room!"

Heather smiled and waved her wand.
"I have a plan!" she said.
As if by magic shining stars
Appeared above the bed.

Now Susie watches stars in bed
To help her get to sleep.
She counts them as they float above,
Instead of counting sheep!

Fairer Princess Sarah

Sarah was the fairest
Royal princess in the land,
And every prince for miles around
Longed to win her hand.

But though she was a picture—
The loveliest you've seen—
Sarah had another side.
She could be REALLY mean!

She wouldn't even let her friends
Touch her things, you see.
"Hands off my pretty toys," she'd shout.
"They all belong to me!

Leave my precious jewels alone . . .
And PLEASE don't touch my dress!
You'll only get it dirty,
And make an awful mess!"

Her friends soon grew quite annoyed.
"Just keep your silly stuff.
We don't want to play with you.
This time we've had enough!"

"How dare they speak to me like that!"
Cried Sarah in surprise.
She ran off to the woods to sulk,
Tears filling up her eyes.

Then Sarah heard a gentle voice.
"There is no need to cry!
Every problem can be solved,"
Said thoughtful Sir MacEye.

"Though your eyes shine like the stars,
And though you may be fair . . .
A good, kind heart means so much more,
So won't you try to share?"

Sarah listened to his words.
"How wise you are," she said.
"I don't need everything I have!
I'll share *my* things instead.

For though I love my pretty toys
And clothes that make me fairer,
I'd rather share them with my friends,
And just be plain old Sarah!"

Jolly Princess Polly

Polly was a funny kind
Of princess, it was thought.
She didn't always act the way
A royal princess ought.

For everywhere that Polly went,
And every time she spoke,
She really couldn't help herself—
OUT would pop a joke!

She snickered at royal gatherings,
And laughed aloud at school.
She giggled in the library
And broke the silence rule!

But though she was tremendous fun,
And made her best friends smile,
She could be most annoying—
Laughing all the while!

"If only Polly made less noise,
And played more quietly,
Instead of laughing fit to burst!"
Complained her family.

Then one day disaster struck.
Poor Polly lost her kitty.
She couldn't even crack a smile!
It really was a pity.

"I wish that you would laugh once more,"
Her friends exclaimed, that night.
"Without your laughter and your jokes,
The palace won't feel right!

If only we could find poor Fluff
And make you smile again.
If we lose your happy face,
Things just won't be the same!"

All at once Sir Dave appeared,
In answer to their wish.
"I found this by the moat," he said,
"Watching all the fish!"

Princess Polly laughed out loud,
To everyone's delight.
"You've found my little Fluff!" she cried,
And kissed the blushing knight.

Now Polly's jolly once again,
So if they're feeling sad,
Her friends just listen to her laugh.
It always makes them glad!